AMALO

(አመሎ)

Written by Rahel Tafese

Translated by Fikru Mosisa

As soon as the sun rises, Grandma Amalo wakes up
and goes out into the field to look for
Moo Moo, the cow.

[ፀሐይ ስትወጣ እማማ አመሎ ላሟ ሙሙን ልትፈልግ ወጣች]

Do you see Moo Moo?
[ሙሙን አየሻት?]

There she is!

[ያቻትና!]

Amalo finds Moo Moo eating the green grass.
Mmm, that's a yummy breakfast

[አረንጓዴ ሳር እየጋጠች አመሎ አገኘቻት፡፡ ምምም
በጣም ይጣፍጣል]

Today, Amalo has a special helper, Bontu, her granddaughter. Bontu loves playing in the green grass with the little calf.

[ዛሬ አመሎ ልዩ ረዳት አላት፤ የልጅ ልጇ ቦንቱ! ቦንቱ በአረንጓዴው ሳር ላይ ከትንሿ ጥጃ ጋር መጫወት ትወዳለች]

Now, it's time to milk Moo Moo. Amalo is so excited to show Bontu how to milk the cow. Moo Moo gives the most delicious milk.

After breakfast, Amalo heads out
into the field of wildflowers. Do you
see the purple and yellow flowers?

ከቁርስ በኋላ ወደ ዱር አበባ! አየሸው ቢጫ አበባ የወይን ጠጅ አበባ!

Then Amalo collects the ripe cherries from the coffee tree.

ከዛ የቡና ፍሬዎችን ለቀመች

Do you see the red cherries in the bag?
አየሻቸው ቀያዮቹን ፍሬዎች ቀረጢት ውስጥ?

Bontu helps with laying
out the cherries in the
sun to dry.

ቦንቱ ፍሬዎቹን ፀሐይ ላይ አሰጣቻቸው

Now, it's lunch time! Amalo goes out into the field to collect wood to build a fire.

ምሳ ሰዓት ደረሰ! አመሎ እንጨት ለመልቀም ወደ ውጪ ወጣች

She chops the wood into little pieces. She's so strong!

እንጨቱን ፈለጦቹው በጣም ጠንካራ ናት!

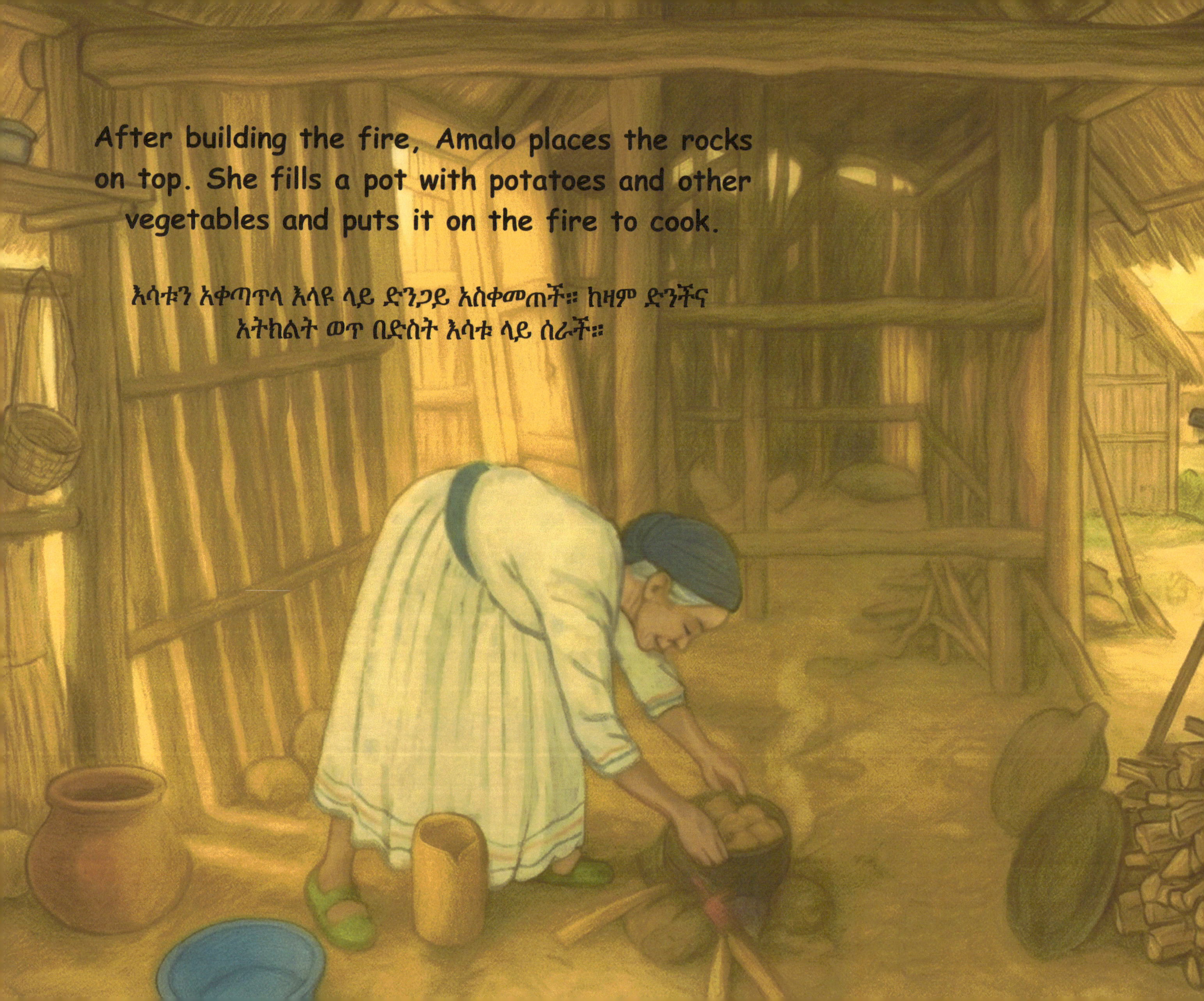

After building the fire, Amalo places the rocks on top. She fills a pot with potatoes and other vegetables and puts it on the fire to cook.

እሳቱን አቀጣጥላ እላዩ ላይ ድንጋይ አስቀመጠች። ከዛም ድንችና አትክልት ወጥ በድስት እሳቱ ላይ ሰራች።

Amalo covers the pot with banana leaves.
ከዛ ድስቱን በመዝ ቅጠል ሸፈነችው

Amalo sits down with her family to enjoy her warm lunch and coffee. It has been a wonderful day!

ምግቡ ሲበስል ከቤተሰቧ ጋር ቁጭ ብላ ትኩስ ምሳ በላች